SANRIO

This book belongs to:

....

Published 2013. Century Books Ltd.
Unit 1, Upside Station Building Solsbro Road,
Torquay, Devon, UK, TQ26FD

books@centurybooksltd.co.uk

CONTENTS

Welcome to the World of SANRIO

Who will you play with today? This annual is bursting with friends that want to say hi! Have you ever wondered which **Sanrio character** is most like you? Work your way across the flowchart, choosing the things that you like best. At the end you'll meet your closest Sanrio match.

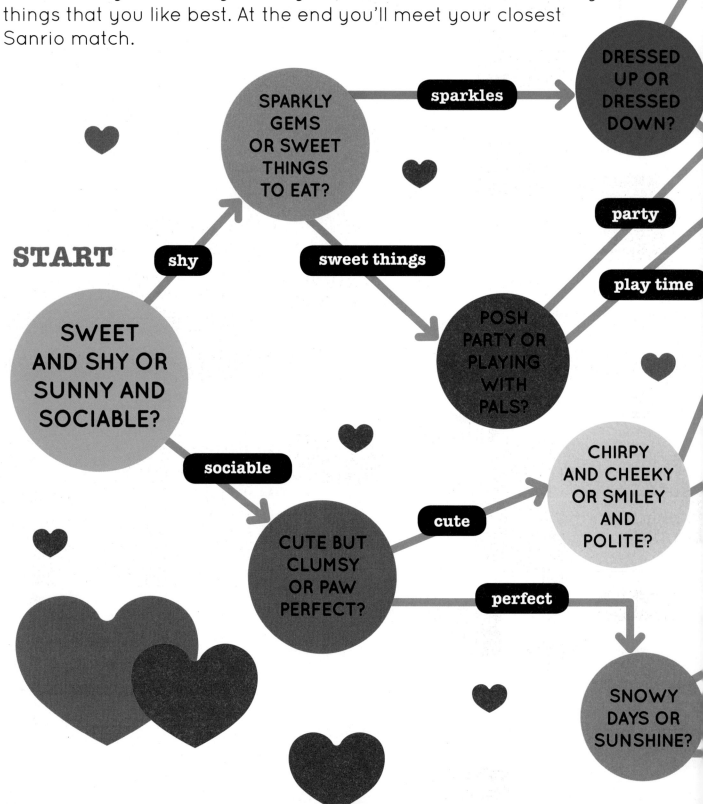

START

SWEET AND SHY OR SUNNY AND SOCIABLE?

shy

sociable

SPARKLY GEMS OR SWEET THINGS TO EAT?

sparkles

sweet things

DRESSED UP OR DRESSED DOWN?

party

play time

POSH PARTY OR PLAYING WITH PALS?

CUTE BUT CLUMSY OR PAW PERFECT?

cute

perfect

CHIRPY AND CHEEKY OR SMILEY AND POLITE?

SNOWY DAYS OR SUNSHINE?

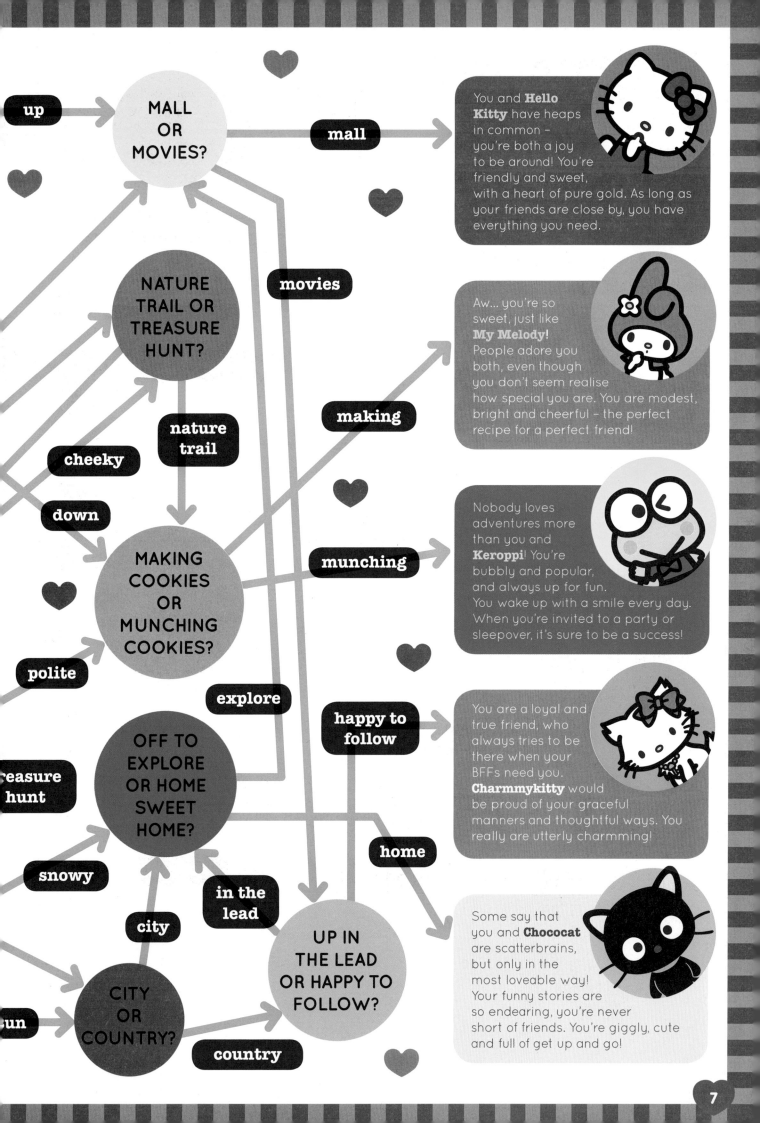

MALL OR MOVIES?

up →

mall →

You and **Hello Kitty** have heaps in common – you're both a joy to be around! You're friendly and sweet, with a heart of pure gold. As long as your friends are close by, you have everything you need.

NATURE TRAIL OR TREASURE HUNT?

movies

making

cheeky

nature trail

Aw... you're so sweet, just like **My Melody!** People adore you both, even though you don't seem realise how special you are. You are modest, bright and cheerful – the perfect recipe for a perfect friend!

down

MAKING COOKIES OR MUNCHING COOKIES?

munching →

Nobody loves adventures more than you and **Keroppi!** You're bubbly and popular, and always up for fun. You wake up with a smile every day. When you're invited to a party or sleepover, it's sure to be a success!

polite

explore

happy to follow →

OFF TO EXPLORE OR HOME SWEET HOME?

You are a loyal and true friend, who always tries to be there when your BFFs need you. **Charmmykitty** would be proud of your graceful manners and thoughtful ways. You really are utterly charming!

reasure hunt

home

snowy

in the lead

city

UP IN THE LEAD OR HAPPY TO FOLLOW?

un

CITY OR COUNTRY?

country

Some say that you and **Chococat** are scatterbrains, but only in the most loveable way! Your funny stories are so endearing, you're never short of friends. You're giggly, cute and full of get up and go!

Hi, Hello Kitty

Everybody loves Hello Kitty – she's sunny, fluffy and fun! The cute kitten always wears a little ribbon on her left ear. Hello Kitty's favourite thing is her mama's home baked apple pie. She and her twin sister Mimmy have lots of friends at school and all over the world. As Hello Kitty says, you can never have too many friends!

BIRTHDAY:	November 1st
LIVES:	In the suburbs of London
HEIGHT:	As tall as 5 apples
COLLECTS:	Small and cute trinkets like candy stars
DREAM:	To be a pianist

Let's make friends!

Fifi

Jodie

Tippy

Joey

Rorry

Tracy

Thomas

Pretty Kitty

Grab your pencil and draw the purrrrfect Kitty cat.

1

Draw a sideways oval, for Kitty's head with a square with round edges underneath it, for her body.

2

Add rounded-corner triangles to the oval for Kitty's ears and a circle and two rounded-corner triangles to create her bow.

3

Next, add her eyes, nose and three whiskers on either side of her head.

4

Then add two arms to the side of her body and draw in her legs and her clothes. To finish, colour her in.

Doodle

Your signature can say a lot about the kind of person you are. Practice yours here.

Fancy yourself as a jewellery designer? Turn these doodles into some fab jewels for Kitty.

Doodle some cute patterns in these hearts.

Help Kitty draw something on her easel.

Nature Spotting

Hello Kitty loves spending the day out in nature with her friends.
Can you find 10 differences between the two pictures?
Circle every one that you spot.

Hello Kitty has a lot of friends
in the forest... like Joey the mouse
and Lorry the squirrel.

Hello Kitty has a lot of friends in the forest... like Joey the mouse and Lozzy the squirrel!

Describe a dream day with your friends here.

....

....

....

....

Don't forget to check your answers on page 92!

BFF Quiz

There's nothing quite like a best friend... they'll be there for you in the good times and the bad and best of all – keep your secrets forever.

Find out if you and your best buddy will be BFF.

1. How long have you been pals for?

a) since forever

b) a couple of years

c) a couple of months

2. Do you ever fall out?

a) sometimes, but only over silly things

b) now and then, but we always make up really quickly

c) most days – we are both really stubborn

3. What would you do if you turned up at a party in the same outfit?

a) nothing – it happens all the time – we're like fashion twins

b) cringe and try and avoid each other

c) she would probably make me leave

4. Do you always keep your friend's secrets?

a) secrets? What secrets? I know nothing…

b) I try but every so often I slip up.

c) of course, unless they're really really juicy!

HELLO KITTY

14

Mostly a's
No doubt about it – you'll be together forever

Mostly b's
Your best buds but also like to do your own thing so may not be BFF and ever

Mostly c's
Most definitely not BFF but your friend is still someone you can have fun with

No.1 Best Friend

Hello Kitty is a brilliant pal and always happy to help.

What makes your friend the perfect pal?

....

....

....

....

....

Lipsmacking Cakes & Cookies

Grab your apron and mixing bowl and impress your friends and family with Kitty's delicious recipes.

Cupcakes

You will need:

- 125g self-raising flour
- 140g butter
- 140g caster sugar
- 3 eggs
- 1 teaspoon of vanilla essence

- Mixing bowl
- Electric mixer or wooden spoon
- Cake tray
- Cake cases

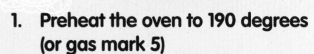

1. Preheat the oven to 190 degrees (or gas mark 5)
2. Beat the eggs and sugar in a bowl until light and fluffy.
3. Next, add the flour, eggs and vanilla essence and beat until smooth.
4. Divide the mixture into your cake cases and cook for about 15 minutes.
5. Remove from the oven and leave to cool.

You can decorate your cakes with all kinds of cool toppings, from icing sugar, chocolate sprinkles, marshmallows, or for a fruiter option add some cream and a strawberry or cherry on top.

HELLO KITTY SWEET BREAK

It's time for a BREAK!

HELLO KITTY CAFE
Cookbook

SWEET MAIN DISHES

Cookies

You will need:

- 250g plain flour
- ½ teaspoon of bicarbonate soda
- 170g unsalted butter (melted)
- 200g brown sugar
- 100g caster sugar
- 1 tablespoon of vanilla extract
- 1 egg
- 1 egg yolk
- 325g chocolate chips

- 2 mixing bowls
- Electric mixer or wooden spoon
- Sieve
- Baking tray and parchment paper

1. Preheat oven to 170 degrees (or gas mark 3) and line some baking trays with parchment or grease them with some butter.
2. Sift together the flour and bicarbonate soda and set aside.
3. In a separate bowl, beat together the butter, caster and brown sugar until well blended, then add in the egg, egg yolk and vanilla extract and beat until creamy.
4. Mix in the sifted ingredients until just blended then stir in the chocolate chips with a wooden spoon.
5. Drop the cookie dough onto the baking tray – each cookie should be about 4 tablespoons of dough. Do not flatten them and space them about 8cm apart.
6. Bake for 15 minutes then remove from the oven and leave to cool.

Party Time

Hello Kitty loves nothing better than throwing a great party. Check out her tips and tricks and plan a perfect party that you and your pals will never forget.

It's a bit cheeky to ask for pressies, but it's always nice to dream about what you might get...

Gift list

Write your wish-list here.

Party theme

What kind of party would you have?

Bowling party ☐
Cinema party ☐
Swimming party ☐
Disco ☐
Restaurant ☐
House party ☐
Karaoke party ☐
Sleepover ☐

Guest list

Top of your to-do list is to compile your guest list. Write down who you'd invite here.

Design your party invite here.

Top Tunes

Make sure you plan your playlist with some great songs to dance and sing along to. What would be your top 10?

1.
2.
3.
4.
5.
6.
7.
8.
9.
10.

Make sure you plan the perfect outfit for your party.

Dress Code

What kind of dress code will your party have?

Smart ☐
Casual ☐
Fancy Dress ☐
Pyjama party ☐

Draw your party outfit here.

Munchies

Don't forget the snacks – no party is complete without loads of goodies to gobble down. What would you have?

Pizza ☐
Chips ☐
Posh sandwiches ☐
Crisps ☐
Popcorn ☐
Ice-cream ☐
Cupcakes ☐
Chocolate ☐
Sausage rolls ☐

Please Come to my Birthday !

Date:
time:
rsvp:

Games

Have loads of great activities planned, like a dance-off or karaoke competition.

Or you could play games like –

- Truth Or Dare, where you take it in turns to either answer a question truthfully or take a dare.
- Truth & Lies, where you take it in turns to tell two true things and one lie about yourself and your friends have got to guess which is the lie.

Two truths and one lie?
My dream is to become a pianist.
I once roller-skated around the world with my friend Chococat... backwards!
I love the colour pink.

Fashion Passion

Make a style statement like Kitty, with these quick and easy fashion makes.

Make some cute Kitty bow-tie hair slides with pasta

1. Take a piece of bow-tie (Farfalle) pasta and paint it red.

2. Leave to dry then add some white spots for a polka-dot look.

3. Once the spots have dried stick the pasta shape on a hair slide and voila – you Kitty and Mimi could be triplets.

Transform an Alice band in seconds

1. Take one boring old Alice band and cover it in glue.

2. Next, wrap some pretty ribbon around it and you're done.

Create some bling-tastic jewellery

1. Measure the distance around your wrist, add 5 cm and cut a piece of thin elastic to size. Choose 10 or so buttons, they can be a mixture of metallic, fabric and plastic.

2. Tie a knot in one end of the elastic and thread the other through a needle.

3. Thread the elastic through the buttonholes, then tie the two ends of your elastic together for a cute and quirky button bracelet.

Turn an old pair of jeans into a handbag

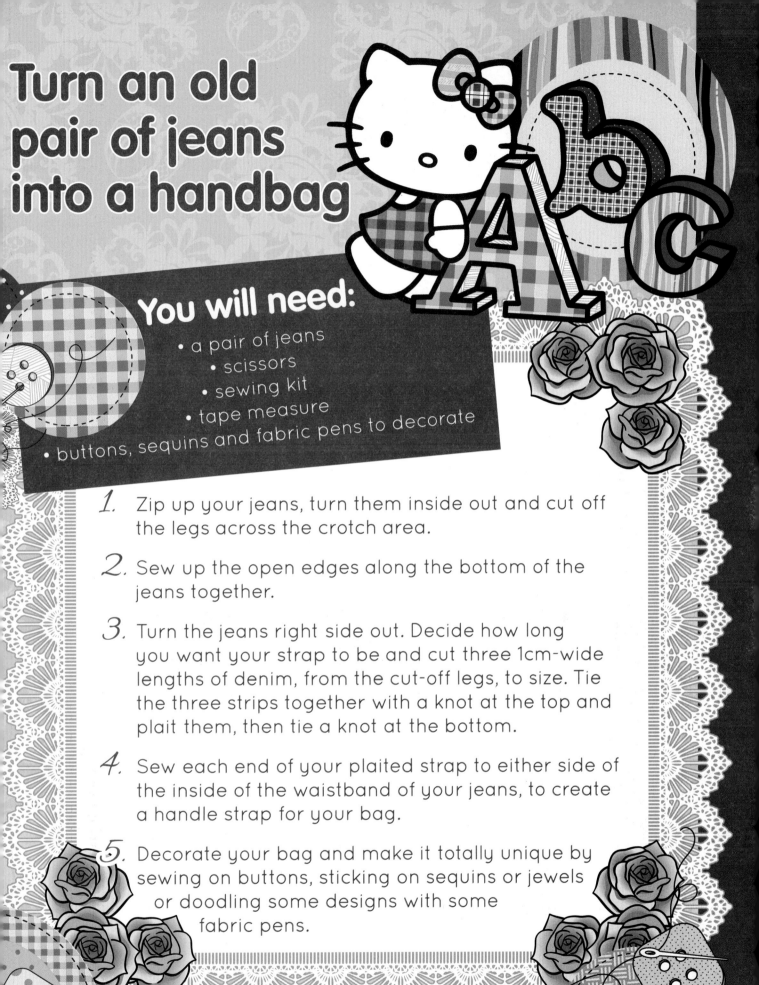

You will need:

- a pair of jeans
- scissors
- sewing kit
- tape measure
- buttons, sequins and fabric pens to decorate

1. Zip up your jeans, turn them inside out and cut off the legs across the crotch area.

2. Sew up the open edges along the bottom of the jeans together.

3. Turn the jeans right side out. Decide how long you want your strap to be and cut three 1cm-wide lengths of denim, from the cut-off legs, to size. Tie the three strips together with a knot at the top and plait them, then tie a knot at the bottom.

4. Sew each end of your plaited strap to either side of the inside of the waistband of your jeans, to create a handle strap for your bag.

5. Decorate your bag and make it totally unique by sewing on buttons, sticking on sequins or jewels or doodling some designs with some fabric pens.

chococat
Says Meow!

Aww... it's Chococat, the friendliest feline on the block! Chococat can be a scatterbrain, but he always means well. His super-sensitive whiskers are brilliant at picking up juicy bits of gossip. Chococat's favourite days are spent playing with his friends in his Choco-choco house.

Let's play!

Cookie-bau

Jellybean

Nutz

The Duckies

BIRTHDAY:	May 10th
BIRTHPLACE:	Chocotown, Colorado
BEST SKILL:	Picking up the latest news on his whisker antennae
HOBBIES:	Playing around the house with his friends
TRADEMARK:	His chocolate-coloured nose

Leafie

Lemonade

Ciffon

Holiday Diary

Fill in the blanks to finish off Chococat's diary using the picture postcards for information.

DEAR DIARY

HAVING THE MOST PURRRRRFECT HOLIDAY IN
                              THE WEATHER HAS BEEN
                                        EVERY DAY.

I HAVE BEEN SURFING AND HAVE FALLEN OFF
MY BOARD   TIMES ALREADY.
I FELL ASLEEP IN THE SUN THE OTHER DAY
AND
I ALSO CAUGHT A FISH / WAVE / COLD.

IN THE AFTERNOON I ENJOYED A BIKE RIDE
THROUGH THE COUNTRYSIDE, IT IS VERY

I CAN'T WAIT TO
COME BACK AGAIN / GO HOME

Choco-crazy!

Grab your pencil and learn how to draw cool cat Chococat...

 1

Draw a large circle with two ears for Chococat's head. Add a smaller (half) circle for his body below.

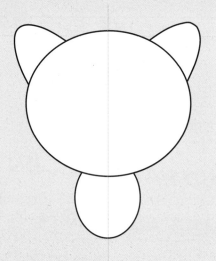

 2

Next, add his arms, legs and tail.

 3

Add two large circles for Chococat's eyes with pupils in, one smaller circle for his nose and two lines either side of his head for his whiskers.

4

To finish, add his collar and colour him in.

Doodle

Draw in some swirly waves for Chococat to surf on.

What do you think Chococat is daydreaming about? Doodle in the dream bubble above.

Use the grid to draw the other half of Chococat's friend, Jellybean.

Weee-heeee! Finish off these fireworks for some amazing explosions!

HOME SWEET HOME

Chococat has created a collage map of Chocotown. Find some bits and pieces and have some fun sticking them in to create your own imaginary town below.

Styled by You...

Have you got a passion for fashion? Let's create some Sanrio couture! Use this page to design a stylish new outfit based on your all-time favourite character.

Tangled Lines

Chococat and his friends have been fishing. Follow the tangled lines to see what each of them have caught.

Don't forget to check your answers on page 92!

Picture Perfect

Oh dear. Chococat has spilled ice cream on his favourite picture. Can you work out which of the pieces below is it covering?

CHOCOCAT

Don't forget to check your answers on page 92!

1

2

3

4

5

CHARMMYKITTY

So sparkly, so pretty... so Charmmykitty

Hello Kitty was thrilled when her papa gave her very own pet! Charmmykitty is an adorable white Persian cat. She is polite, dainty and well-behaved, always ready to listen to everything that Hello Kitty says. Charmmy has a pet of her own, too. Sugar the hamster is cheeky and naughty, but he never leaves the kitty-cat's side.

BIRTHDAY: October 1st
LIVES: With Hello Kitty
CHARM POINT: Her lace-trimmed bow – a present from Kitty
TRADEMARK: The key to Kitty's jewellery box that she wears around her neck
FAVOURITE THING: Anything bright and sparkly

Pet perfection...

Mille-feuille

Tiramisu

Sugar

Charmmy's sister Honey Cute

Chocolat

Biscuit

My Wonderful Week!

Charmmy Kitty is so busy this week – look at all of these engagements! She would love to share her schedule with someone. Are you free? Read Charmmy Kitty's writing, then draw a portrait of yourself into each frame. What will you wear for each date? Give yourself seven stunning new looks!

Monday
SUGAR'S BIRTHDAY PARTY

Tuesday
A VISIT TO THE FLOWER SHOW

Wednesday
FRUIT PICKING WITH HELLO KITTY

Thursday
TEA AT THE ICE-CREAM PARLOUR

When you have finished each portrait, colour it in. Why not add a sprinkling of glitter to a few of your favourites?

Friday
SPA DATE WITH HONEY CUTE

Saturday
FUN DAY AT THE PET SHOP

Sunday
BAKE CUPCAKES WITH ALL OF MY FRIENDS

It's what's inside that counts...

It's all very well looking pretty as a picture, but it's what kind of person you are that really matters.

FUN **SWEET**

LOVING

KIND

LOYAL

Check out this personality pie chart for Charmmy Kitty, then take the test to see what you're made of.

You

LOVING

REBELLIOUS

LOYAL

NAUGHTY

KIND

MOODY

FUN

ENERGETIC

SWEET

FRIENDLY

BOSSY

DARING HAPPY

ADVENTUROUS

CARING

What kind of person are you?

1. If you were an animal what would you be?
- a) a tiger
- b) a penguin
- c) a mouse

I would be a hamster so I could be just like my friend Sugar.

2. If you could be anyone in the world you would be…
- a) a world leader
- b) myself
- c) invisible

I would be a Pirate Princess and I would help the poor of course.

3. If you were a colour what would you be?
- a) red
- b) green
- c) white

If I was a colour I would be pink.

4. If you were a type of weather you would be…
- a) a lightning storm
- b) a sunny day
- c) fog

Mmmmm. I would want to be ice-cream, just because I love it!

5. If you were a type of food you would be…
- a) pizza
- b) BBQ food
- c) a sandwich

MOSTLY A'S
You like to stand out from the crowd, be brave, bold and adventurous and want everyone to like you.

MOSTLY B'S
You like to go with the flow, have fun and keep yourself and everyone around you happy.

MOSTLY C'S
You can lack confidence and often get embarrassed but you're always happy and a great friend.

Cute Kitty

Follow the instructions below to create a cute and cuddly Charmmy Kitty of your own.

1

Start with an egg shape for the head and add a body, which should be a bit like a mushroom stem.

2

Draw in her furry cheeks, ears and bow.

3

Add two small circles for eyes, a cute button nose and three whiskers on either side of Charmmy Kitty's face.

4

Draw in her fluffy tail, add a fluffy outline to her body and draw in her legs. To finish, colour in her bow.

Doodle

Turn these squiggles into some pretty bows for Charmmy Kitty.

What do you think Charmmy Kitty is daydreaming about? Doodle in the dream bubble above.

Doodle Charmmy Kitty some new bling jewellery to go with her key necklace.

Finish off the bunting above with some cool patterns.

39

Flower Garden

Charmmy Kitty loves pretty flowers. Draw lots of flowers for her below and colour them in.

Trail of Hearts

Help Charmmy Kitty follow the trail of hearts to get to a party that she has been invited to. She can only go in straight lines in the following colour order:

pink – green – orange – purple

End

Start

Don't forget to check your answers on page 92!

41

MAKE WAY FOR Badtz-Maru™

There's no one quite like Badtz-Maru... and he doesn't care who knows it! The tearaway penguin lives with his mama and his pinball-loving papa in Gorgeous Town. When he's not causing mischief, Badtz-Maru walks the streets with his snap-happy pet croc, Pochi.

BIRTHDAY: April 1st (April Fool's Day)
BIRTHPLACE: Oahu, Hawaii
LIVES: Gorgeous Town
DREAM: To be a company president!
HOBBIES: Collecting photos of bad guy movie stars
Beating up goody-goodies
FAVOURITE FOOD: The best sushi money can buy

It's a Badtz Badtz world...

Pochi

Pandaba

Hana-maru

Try out Badtz-Maru's brain-bending puzzles.

1. Secret Code

Badtz★Maru

loves texting his friends secret messages. To make sure nobody else can understand them though, he's come up with a secret code. Can you crack it and work out what his texts say.

A B C
D E F
G H I
J K L
M N O
P Q R
S T U
V W X
Y Z

Meet me at the

SKATE

PARK

in

ONE

HOUR XO

The answer to

HOME

WORK

question

NUMBER

2 is 100. XO

Let's

buy

Chococat a

NEW

COLLAR

for

his

birthday. XO

Last

night I

dreamt

I was a

cowboy

XO

2. Double Trouble!

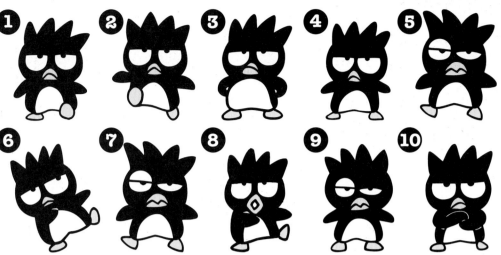

Can you spot 2 Badtz-Marus that are exactly the same?

3. Punchlines

Badtz-Maru loves making his friends laugh but he's forgotten the punchlines to these penguin jokes. Can you match them up for him?

1. Why does a penguin never do what he sets out to do?

2. How does a penguin feel at lunchtime?

3. What do you call a penguin in the desert?

4. What do you call a happy penguin?

d) pen-grin

a) lost

b) he always gets cold feet

c) peckish

4. Fave Food

Cross out all the letters that appear three times to reveal Badtz-Maru's fave food.

Q W E R T Y O S P A D F G J U K L Z
X C V B N S M Q W E R T Y O P A D
H F G J K L Z X C V B N M Q W E R T
Y O P A D F I G J K L Z X C V B N M

5. P is for....

How many animals can you think of beginning with the letter P?
Here's some to get you started...

Penguin ....

Polar bear ....

Poodle ....

Pelican ....

....

....

....

....

....

....

Don't forget to check your answers on page 92!

BADtz·MARU

1

Draw an oval for Badtz-Maru's head, with four spikes for his hair and a rounded-edged square for his body.

2

Add in two half circles for his eyes, his black pupils and his beak.

3

Add in his little wings and flat feet.

4

Draw in his tummy and colour him in.

Doodle

Doodle some backgrounds to these
Badtz-Maru action shots!

Close your eyes and see if you can draw a line with your
pencil from Badtz-Maru's bow and arrow to hit the target.

Doodle some weird and wacky aliens in the empty space ships.

Bike Challenge

Prove to
Badtz-Maru
that you can!

I bet you
can't design
a better bike
than mine...

Design
your
racing
badge.

Badtz-Maru

Picture Perfect

Can you work out what Badtz-Maru has spotted through his binoculars?

1

2

3

Don't forget to check your answers on page 92!

4

5

Badtz-Maru

1 ....

2 ....

3 ....

4 ....

5 ....

Oh dear! One of Badtz-Maru's friends have become jumbled up! Who do you think it is?

....

IT'S KEROPPI

If there's an adventure to be had in the big blue of Donut Pond, Keroppi will jump in with both froggy feet! Keroppi is bouncy, bubbly and full of fun. He's one of three triplets that live happily with their parents in Kerokero house. Keroppi and his friends love playing games, especially baseball and boomerang.

Introducing the frog-fabulous Hasunoue family...

BIRTHDAY:	July 10th
LIVES:	Donut Pond
DREAM:	To have bigger and better adventures!
HOBBIES:	Swimming and singing (but not at the same time!)
BEST FRIEND:	Den Den the slow little snail

PAPA

MAMA

PIKKI

KOROPPI

Cool Café

What do you like to order when you go to a café?

- Coffee ☐
- Tea ☐
- Soft drink ☐
- Fruit juice ☐
- Smoothie ☐
- Breakfast ☐
- Cake ☐
- Cookie ☐
- Ice-cream ☐
- Hot dog ☐
- Burger ☐
- Fries ☐

If you had your own café, what would you call it? Design a café logo here.

Now for the cakes, draw some delicious toppings on these cupcakes.

What would you put on the menu?

Daily Menu

....
....
....
....
....
....
....
....
....
....

Think up some cool-sounding drinks using the words below.

ice ....

cool ....

berry ....

smoothie ....

fizzy ....

bubbly ....

juice ....

hot ....

chocca chocca ....

organic ....

lip-smacking ....

thirst-quenching ....

guzzling ....

52

All good café owners know that how your café looks inside, is almost as important as the food you serve.

What would be special about your café?

Sweet treats ☐
Organic food ☐
Healthy eating ☐
Internet café ☐
Big breakfasts ☐
Gourmet food ☐
Outside tables ☐
Magazines and books to read ☐
Ice-cream parlour ☐
Music and a dukebox ☐
Football table ☐
Pool table ☐

Design some cool patterns for your tablecloths here.

Placemats

Serviette

Plate

Cutlery

Now doodle some designs for your tableware.

Cup

Bowl

Teacup

Hippity Hoppity Puzzles
KERoPPI

Don't forget to check your answers on page 92!

is ready for a brand new adventure! Can you leapfrog from lily pad to lily pad, completing the quizzes along the way? Try and crack all six in under six minutes.

Odd object out

Look at these pictures. Can you circle the odd-one-out in each row?

1.

2.

Croaky counting

Study the picture. How many Keroppis can you count?

Letter jumble

Unscramble the letters to reveal the name of Keroppi's favourite rain charm.

3.

UETURERT

....

54

Memories of Donut Pond

Look at the picture and count to ten, then cover it up with your hand. Can you answer all of the questions?

1. What colour is Keroppi's scarf?

....

2. How many trees did you count?

....

3. How is Teruteru getting around on the ice?

....

4. What have the friends made on the side of the pond?

....

4.

新年を
むかえる！

Crazy for Keroppi

5.

Write down at least three new words, only taking the letters from the title to the left.

1. ....

2. ....

3. ....

What's the longest word you can make?

....

Gone fishin'

Keroppi is floating on his favourite lily pad, waiting for a bite! Circle three differences between the pictures.

6.

55

KEROPPI Time

Learn how to draw everyone's fave green frog – Keroppi.

1

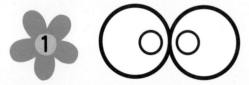

Draw two big circles for Keroppi's eyes, making sure the left eye overlaps the right one. Add two pupils in each circle.

2

Draw a half oval shape underneath the circles for Keroppi's face and add two small circles for his cheeks and a v-shape line for his mouth.

3

Next draw his body shape and add in his arms and legs as shown.

4

To finish, colour him in. Don't forget his bow tie!

Doodle

Check out the funny faces Keroppi is pulling. Can you doodle some eyes and different mouth shapes on the faces below, so Keroppi looks...

in lurve   *angry*   *happy*

What do you think Keroppi is daydreaming about? Doodle in the dream bubble below.

Doodle some new clothes for Keroppi.

Doodle lots of little fish

GAME ON

Keroppi has challenged his friend Keroleen to a race across Donut Pond. Find a friend and pick a character to see who can make it across first.

How to play

- For two players or more
- Use a coin for your counter
- Take it in turns to move across the board. There is no dice, each go just close your eyes and point to a number on the Number Jumbler on the right.
- Follow any instructions you land on.
- First one across the pond wins. Anyone who cheats will be disqualified!

1 START

2 slip on snail slime, miss a go

3 stop to catch a fish, miss a go

4 hop on one leg for ten seconds and leap forward one space

5 fall in the pond, go back to the start

6 leap forward two spaces

7 sing a song and have another go

8 say 'Charmmy Kitty is very pretty' really fast and leap forward one space

9 get bitten by a crab, miss a go

10 name three animals beginning with the letter C and leap forward one space

11 stop to have a drink, miss a go

12 leap forward three spaces

58

SANRIO *your world!*

Sanrio-style is as simple as 1, 2, 3

- Design a *Sanrio* comic strip or graphic novel.
- Create a unique *Sanrio* repeat print, then cover your text books and diary.
- Make *Sanrio* bookmarks and a sign for your bedroom door!
- Use fabric pens to *customize* your pencil case.

Animé flip book

Want to see Keroppi dance? Easy peasy! An animated flipbook is a brilliant way to bring Sanrios character to life.

YOU WILL NEED
- A deck of index cards
- Black fine-tipped pen
- Pencils or crayons for colouring
- Bulldog clip

1 Turn the top card so that it is landscape in format, then draw a picture of Keroppi. Try to keep your drawing as simple as possible as you will need to copy it lots of times.

2 Put the top card in front of you, then draw another picture of Keroppi on the next one. Take care to move his pose on ever so slightly. Don't worry if your drawing isn't a completely perfect match to the first – as long as Sam is in the roughly the same position your animation will work.

3 Carry on drawing on more index cards, until you have at least 25. Make Keroppi do something simple such as move left to right, or hop.

IT IS A GOOD IDEA TO NUMBER YOUR CARDS SO THAT THEY DON'T GET MIXED UP.

4 When all of your cards are finished, colour the drawings in. Shade each one the same so that your animation will flow nicely.

5 Stack your cards in a neat pile, then use a bulldog clip to hold the left hand edge together. Flick the cards with your right hand and enjoy!

Froggy Friends

Copy Keroppi and his best friends in the bottom grid using the grid above and then colour them both in.

KUROMI ™
CHEEKY BUT CHARMING

Watch out – My Melody's rowdy rival Kuromi is coming this way! The punky bunny is the leader of a tricycle-peddling bikie gang called 'Kuromi's 5'. There's nothing to be frightened of however, beneath that black joker's hat is a cute girly-girl that's bursting to get out! Kuromi is a cheeky, free spirit who just wants to have some fun.

BIRTHDAY: October 31st
SECRET: She's tough on the outside, but girly on the inside
Kuromi has a soft spot for cute guys
DREAM: Keeping a diary
HOBBIES: Reading romance novels
FAVOURITE FOOD: Pickled onions

CHECK OUT KUROMI'S BUDDIES...

NYAMI

WANMI

CHUMI

BAKU

KONMI

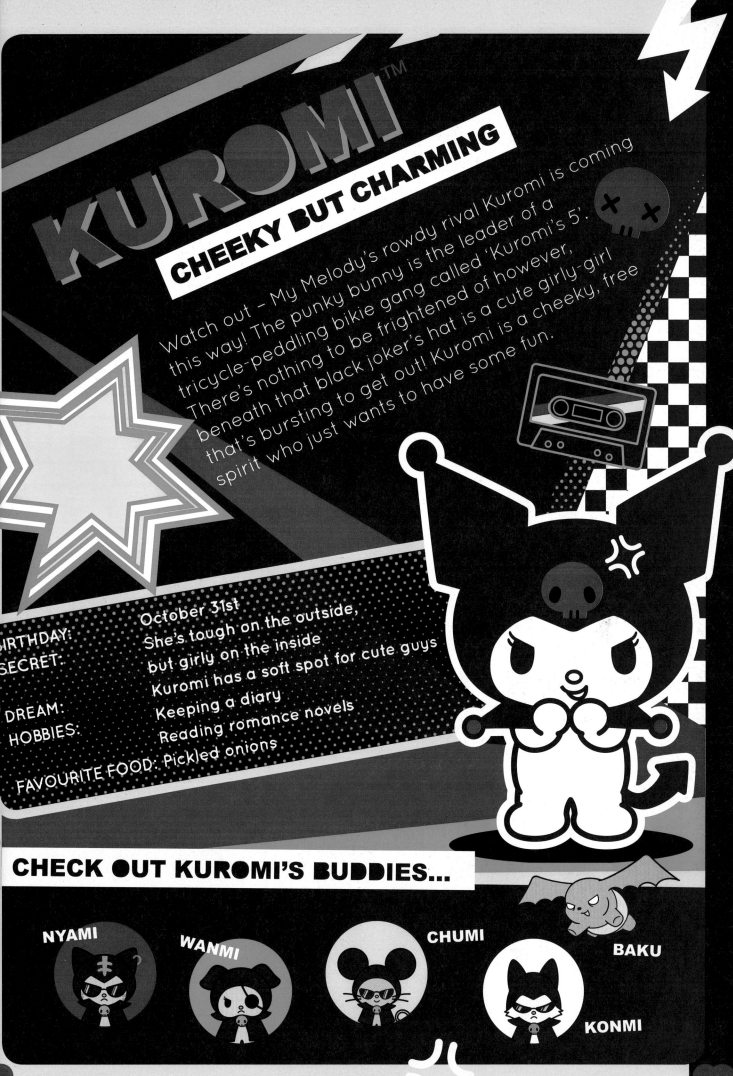

TERROR TRAIL

Oh no! Kuromi is stuck inside a haunted house. Help her find her way out of this spook-tacular maze.

SAFE!

How many cobwebs can you spot?	
How many spiders can you see?	
Count up the bats.	

See answers on page 93

Can you fit the words below into the grid.

LETTERS
bat
cat

LETTERS
frog
~~moon~~

LETTERS
ghost
~~witch~~

6 LETTERS
goblin
spider
shadow
spooky
cobweb

7 LETTERS
haunted
vampire

8 LETTERS
cauldron

10 LETTERS
broomstick

Ha ha!

What does a witch ask for in a hotel?

Broom service!

Ha ha!

What's a ghost's favourite fruit?

BOOberries!

Don't forget to check your answers on page 93!

65

KUROMI CREEPOVER

Having your BFFs over anytime soon? Why not shake things up by hosting a creepover? It's just a sleepover with a sprinkling of spookiness thrown in! These pages are packed full of creepover ideas – it's freaky good fun!

KUROMI™

CREATE THE INVITATIONS

Use black paper and silver pens to design a scroll invitation for each of your guests. Tear the edges of each invite so that it looks ragged and old, then pop a plastic spider or bug inside when you wrap it up.

SET THE SCENE

For one night only, your house needs to look spooky, dark and unwelcoming! Paint cereal boxes grey and write your friends' names on them. Prop these up in your front garden to make tombstones. Dig out your old Hallowe'en decorations, then drape your bedroom in cobwebs. Turn out the lights and use candles instead.

MAKE A FEARSOME FEAST

Be creative with your snacks and drinks. Blood orange juice makes a grim fruit punch, especially if there's a severed plastic finger or a pair of eyeballs floating on the top. If you want to cook a main meal, ask your parents to help you make spaghetti and tomato sauce, then present it to your friends as blood and guts! DON'T FORGET to save some treats to serve at midnight, too...

MURDEROUS MAKEOVER

Get some face paints in, stock up on hair spray and find some black and scarlet nail polishes. Take turns to give each other deathly makeovers. Think white zombie faces, backcombed hair and sunken, hollow eyes. Give a prize to the most gruesome guest.

SCARY MOVIE SHOW

Get your DVDs ready in advance. Take the time to choose movies that will make your guests squeal with excitement, not scream in fright. No one wants nightmares!

THE CURSE OF THE ZOMBIE

Sit everyone in a circle, turn off the light then tell a story about a zombie that came to a sticky end. Describe how his cursed body was cut up into different pieces, describing each part in horrible detail. Mention the zombie's heart, then pass around a plate with a soft pepper. Talk about his eyes, then pass a bowl with two peeled grapes round the circle, asking your guests to touch for themselves. Use popcorn for his teeth, a dried apricot for his tongue and anything else you can find!

SPOOKY SURPRISES

Why not give your friends a little more than they bargained for? A few carefully planned games and surprises will make them giggle all night long. Persuade your dad to jump out of a closet in the middle of a silly ghost story or make crazy masks for everyone to wear.

FUN BY FLASHLIGHT

When it gets dark, head out into the garden with your torches. Go stargazing, then sit in a circle and share spooky stories. Why not set up a treasure hunt with creepy clues for your guests to follow?

THREE OF THE WORST CREEPOVER GAMES

1 WINK MURDER
Choose one person to be the murderer, then sit in a circle. The murderer can kill people in the ring by secretly winking at them. How many can they murder before they get caught?

2 MAD MUMMIES
Get into pairs, then time how long it takes to roll each other up with toilet paper – the quickest mummy wins!

3 BAD BOBBING
Fill a bowl with spray cream, then drop some gummy worms and creepy crawlies inside. Tie your hair back, then pick up as many as you can without using your hands!

DON'T FORGET TO ASK YOUR PARENTS BEFORE INVITING YOUR FRIENDS OVER! A FUN CREEPOVER SHOULD BE SPINE-TINGLING, NOT TEETH-CHATTERINGLY SCARY – IF ANYONE GETS FREAKED OUT, STOP THE GAME AND PLAY SOMETHING ELSE INSTEAD.

KOOLIO KUROMI

Follow the instructions below to create a Kuromi masterpiece.

1 Draw a big circle for Kuromi's head and add two lines to the top. Then draw her body with an arm and tail line.

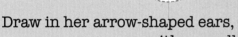

2 Draw in her arrow-shaped ears, with a small circle on the top of each one and the outline of her hood across her face.

3 Draw in Kuromi's eyes, nose and mouth and add the skull to her hood and a collar around her neck.

4 To finish, add her arms, legs and tail and colour her in.

68

Doodle...

... some new designs on Kuromi's hat.

Doodle some music notes for Kuromi to rock to.

"I rock!"

Turn these squiggles into some clouds, hearts and skulls – Kuromi style!

GRAFFITI SPOTTING

Kuromi is having fun with graffiti. Look closely, can you spot ten differences between these 2 pictures?

Don't forget to check your answers on page 93!

Picture Perfect

Can you work out which spooky shadow is Kuromi's?

Kuromi

1

2

3

4

5

Don't forget to check your answers on page 93!

Meet
My Melody®

My Melody is a shy little forest bunny with cute floppy ears and a snowy white tail. She is honest, good-natured and true. My Melody can often be spotted skipping in and out of the trees on her way to Grandma's house. Just look out for her cute hood and basket of scrummy things!

Friends mean everything...

Flatto

Piano

Risu

BIRTHDAY: January 18th
LIVES: A forest in Mari Land
BEST TREASURE: The bright red hood her grandma made for her
HOBBIES: Baking cookies with Mama
Picking posies of flowers
FAVOURITE FOOD: Almond pound cake

Sweet Melody

Follow the steps below to draw Sanrio cutie – My Melody.

1

Draw a sideways oval, for Melody's head with a square with round edges underneath it, for her body.

2

Draw in Melody's ears, bow or flower and a smaller circle to create her hood.

3

Add circles for her eyes and nose and a little curved smile for her mouth.

4

To finish, add the collar of her cape, her arms and legs and colour her in.

Doodle

Draw in some waves for My Melody and Flat to swim through.

Doodle some patterns in these stars.

My Melody is dressing up for Halloween. Add some spooky spiders and cobwebs to her bunny ears.

My Melody and her friends love to relax in the sunshine. Doodle some cool sunglasses on their faces.

My Melody
Strawberry Wonderland

My Melody adores strawberries – they're sweet and scrummy, just like her! The next time that you have a basketful, give these recipes a try.

Strawberry sundaes

Find a set of tall sundae dishes, then stack them up with sweet treats! It's fun to experiment with different layers and flavours.

To make four sundaes, you will need:

300g strawberries
20g icing sugar
150g crushed chocolate chip cookies
250g vanilla ice cream
Aerosol whipped cream
Mini marshmallows or chocolate flakes to decorate

1. Wash and hull all of the strawberries, then separate out one third to make the strawberry sauce sundae topping.

2. Put this fruit into a bowl and use a handheld blender to pulse the pieces together. Push the strawberry pulp through a sieve to get rid of all the pips. Stir the icing sugar into the pulp to sweeten it, then put the sauce to one side.

3. Take out your sundae dishes and drop half of the remaining hulled strawberries at the bottom of each. Take care to share the fruit out evenly.

4. Next divide up the crushed chocolate chip cookies, putting a quarter in each dish.

5. Follow the crushed cookies with a layer of vanilla ice cream, then add the rest of the hulled strawberries on top.

6. Give your can of aerosol cream a good shake, then spray some on the top of each sundae. Carefully drizzle over the pulped strawberry sauce and sprinkle over a handful of mini marshmallows. Find four spoons and share the sundaes out with your favourite friends!

Strawberries are sweet and yummy.

Strawberry custard ices

These thirst-quenching ices are luscious and sweet! When you want to eat them, run the moulds under a warm tap for a few seconds – the lollies will come out perfectly.

To make at least four ice lollies, you will need:
400g strawberries
150g ready-to-eat pot of custard

1. Carefully wash the strawberries and hull them.

2. Place the fruit in a food processor and blend it thoroughly.

3. Pour the blended strawberries into a sieve and push them through into a bowl. All of the pips should be left behind.

4. Mix the ready-made custard into the smooth strawberry pulp and stir.

5. Pour the mixture into clean lolly moulds and pop them in the freezer. Allow eight hours for the ices to set.

Feeling arty?

Cut a strawberry shape out of red card, then snip a stalk out of green paper and glue it in place. Stick on scarlet sequins here and there or little clusters of glitter to make a cutie-fruitie decoration for your bedroom wall!

Why not...?

Sprinkle a handful of strawberries on your breakfast.

Dip some in chocolate, pop them on cocktail sticks pushed into a grapefruit and then chill in the fridge. The result? Strawberry-choco heaven!

Plant a strawberry patch in your garden, or grow a single plant in a pot.

Find a pretty basket and go strawberry picking with your friends.

WOW!

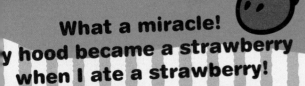

What a miracle! My hood became a strawberry when I ate a strawberry!

Style Queen

Calling all fashionistas... find out what's hot and what's not for you and your fave Sanrio buddies.

Fave celeb style:

Fave friends' style:

Fave Sanrio character's style:

My fashion wish list...
1.
2.
3.
4.
5.

Fave items in my wardrobe:
1.
2.
3.
4.
5.

Steal Their Style

Think
pink and pastels and accessorise your look with cute bows and ribbons, like Kitty and Charmmy.

Smart
Keroppi-style nautical stripes are always a winner for a stylish look.

Rock
Kuromi's look by wearing all black with cool skull motifs

Hats off to Kuromi and My Melody – those bunnies sure love a nice hat. Find out what kind of hat would suit you.

Heart-shaped face
Most hats suit you but wear them tilted to one side.
Try a fedora for ultimate chic.

Square face
Choose hats that have curvy or floppy lines that will soften your face. A cute woolly beanie will be just the job.

Oval face
You look great in lots of hats, but avoid tall, narrow ones. Top your look with a Panama or wide-brimmed hat.

The Sanrio girls love getting dressed up. Work out whose style is most like yours.

Do you go totally ga ga over crazy outfits?		
YES	NO	MAYBE

Are you always late cos you change your mind about what to wear?		
YES	NO	MAYBE

Would you rather wear eyeliner than lipgloss?		
YES	NO	MAYBE

Are your fave jeans so old they should be in a museum?		
YES	NO	MAYBE

Do you hate being a fashion victim?		
YES	NO	MAYBE

Do you prefer wearing black to any other colour?		
YES	NO	MAYBE

You answered mostly YES
Kuromi is your style twin. You like to stand out and look different and love dramatic and dark looks to match your mood.

You answered mostly NO
Charmmy Kitty would love to go shopping with you – you keep up with all the latest styles and always know what's in fashion.

You answered mostly MAYBE
Like Kitty, you're bang on trend but not a slave to fashion and like to experiment with your own style.

Test your fashion know-how and circle True or False for the following style statements...

See answers on page 93

1. Black clothes are hot – literally, as they attract the heat.

   True / False

2. The Beanie hat was invented by Arabella Beanie-Weanie.

   True / False

3. Thousands of years ago cavemen wore miniskirts.

   True / False

4. There are 40 fashion weeks a year, held all over the world.

   True / False

5. People in Australia wear their shoes on their heads.

   True / False

6. High-waisted trousers make your legs look longer.

   True / False

7. Ancient Eygptians use to wear makeup to protect their eyes from infection.

   True / False

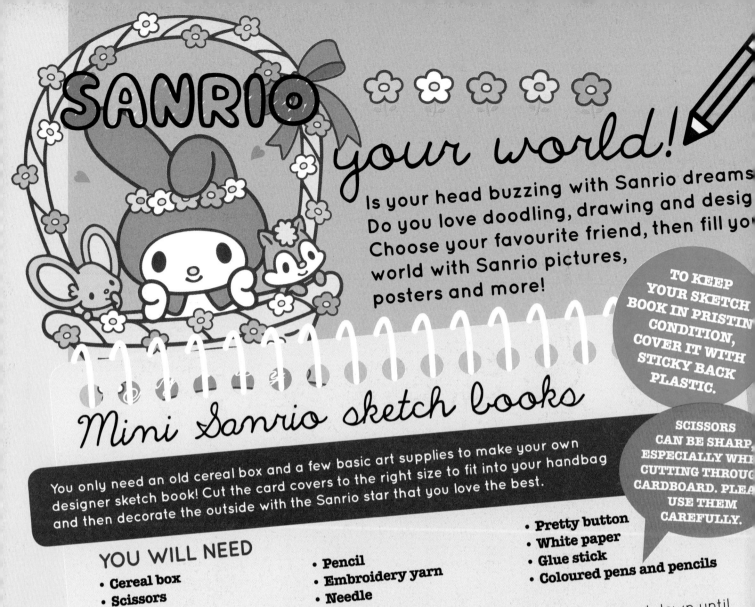

SANRIO your world!

Is your head buzzing with Sanrio dreams
Do you love doodling, drawing and desig
Choose your favourite friend, then fill yo
world with Sanrio pictures,
posters and more!

TO KEEP YOUR SKETCH BOOK IN PRISTIN CONDITION, COVER IT WITH STICKY BACK PLASTIC.

SCISSORS CAN BE SHARP, ESPECIALLY WHI CUTTING THROUG CARDBOARD. PLEA USE THEM CAREFULLY.

Mini Sanrio sketch books

You only need an old cereal box and a few basic art supplies to make your own designer sketch book! Cut the card covers to the right size to fit into your handbag and then decorate the outside with the Sanrio star that you love the best.

YOU WILL NEED

- Cereal box
- Scissors
- Ruler
- Pencil
- Embroidery yarn
- Needle
- Pretty button
- White paper
- Glue stick
- Coloured pens and pencils

1 Unfold the cereal box then cut out one of the flat sides. Trim the card down until it is the right size to form the back cover of your sketch book. Carefully fold the card in half so that the coloured side is hidden in the middle.

2 Carefully thread some embroidery yarn through a needle and then sew the button onto the front of the notebook about halfway down. Knot the yarn at the back, but leave around 30cm hanging at the front. You will use this later to wrap round your notebook when you want to close it.

3 Cover the inside of the folded card with glue stick, then lay a sheet of paper on top to hide the coloured printing. Trim the paper out so that it fits exactly.

4 Take 10 sheets of paper, then trim them down so that they are at least 2cm smaller that the cover of the sketchbook. Fold the sheets in half.

5 Thread some more embroidery yarn, then carefully stitch the folded blank paper into the card cover. Start at the top of the spine and work down.

6 Stick a sheet of white paper over the outside cover of the sketchbook and trim it to fit. Open the pages of the book and lay it flat.

7 Use some pens and pencils to decorate your sketchbook. This is the time to have fun and experiment! Fill the front cover with a large portrait of your favourite Sanrio character, or create a funky repeat pattern.

Colourful Melody

My Melody appears to be missing some colour. Help her out and make her as colourful as you can. Don't forget to draw some patterns in the background and use lots of pink...

I ♥ SANRIO

Take a peep into your special Sanrio photo album! It's packed full of happy snaps of Hello Kitty and her friends having fun. Can you write a caption for every shot? The first one has been written to get you started. Find a pen and get scribbling!

Badtz-Maru enjoying his winter holidays. The plucky penguin has conquered the ski jump!

....
....

....
....

....
....

SANRIO BOX BONANZA

Uh-oh. These pages have gone cube crazy. Find a pen then work your way down the quiz, ticking the right box every time. These brainteasers will test even the most dedicated Sanrio fan. Don't be square – join in the fun.

Don't forget to check your answers on page 93!

1

Hello Kitty is as tall as 5 apples.

TRUE ☐
FALSE ☐

2

Chococat was named after his chocolate-coloured nose.

TRUE ☐
FALSE ☐

3

Chococat's pal is called Jellybelly.

TRUE ☐
FALSE ☐

4

Charmmy Kitty's fluffy friend Sugar is a hamster.

TRUE ☐
FALSE ☐

5

Badtz-Maru's birthday is on April Fools' Day.

TRUE ☐
FALSE ☐

6

My Melody loves baking.

TRUE ☐
FALSE ☐

7

My Melody lives in Fairyland Swamp

TRUE ☐
FALSE ☐

8

Keroppi hates swimming.

TRUE ☐
FALSE ☐

9

Kuromi rocks on the guitar.

TRUE ☐
FALSE ☐

10

Kuromi loves dressing in girly pink.

TRUE ☐
FALSE ☐

11

Kitty has a twin sister called Kimmy.

TRUE ☐
FALSE ☐

12

Keroppi is a triplet.

TRUE ☐
FALSE ☐

HOW DID YOU DO?

0-4

There's still some work to do, but don't feel Badtz! It's time to think outside the box and perfect your puzzling skills.

5-9

Your ticking instincts are looking good. But you could do with learning a few more Sanrio facts. What are you waiting for? Hop to it!

10-12

Congratulations, you officially rock at this. Take a moment to give yourself a HUGE pat on the back and enjoy the glory!

PICKED and MIXED!

Roll up roll up. Are you ready to try your luck with this super-sized wordsearch game? All your fave Sanrio characters want to play too and are hidden, along with their Sanrio family and friends, in the giant letter square opposite.

BADTZ-MARU	HELLO KITTY	
CHARMMY KITTY	JELLYBEAN	
CHOCOCAT	JOEY	MY MELODY
COOKIE-BAU	KEROLEEN	PANDABA
DEN DEN	KEROPPI	POCHI
FLAT GANTA	KUROMI	THOMAS
HANA-MARU	LORRY	TRACY

SANRIO CHARACTERS

Take your time and look closely – the names could be hiding in any direction. Check the vertical, horizontal and diagonal lines, looking forward and backwards.

Don't forget to check your answers on page 93!

```
Y  C  I  K  Q  I  O  Z  Q  N  H  X  U  R  A
D  T  R  W  H  T  M  E  W  F  C  Q  N  O  B
C  P  T  C  J  O  E  Y  Y  Z  L  D  S  E  A
R  G  O  I  J  E  L  L  Y  B  E  A  N  K  D
I  P  C  C  K  U  K  S  M  U  W  C  T  E  N
O  P  Q  C  T  Y  A  U  R  L  H  R  Y  R  A
A  J  P  R  O  M  M  A  R  O  O  T  T  O  P
W  T  A  O  O  O  M  M  C  O  T  U  T  L  M
K  C  N  H  R  Z  K  O  R  U  M  V  I  E  Y
Y  V  T  T  T  E  C  I  K  A  I  I  K  E  M
Y  N  P  D  G  A  K  C  E  V  H  O  O  N  E
L  X  A  V  T  S  B  I  Z  B  G  C  L  T  L
N  B  U  R  A  M  A  N  A  H  A  R  L  O  O
D  E  N  D  E  N  Y  R  R  O  L  U  E  R  D
G  J  X  N  H  O  E  X  Y  J  D  O  H  X  Y
```

Quick 'n' cute QUIZ

How well do you know the world of Sanrio? It's a place full of friendship, laughter and fun. Find a pen, then put yourself to the test. The word and picture questions in this cute quiz are sure to keep you on your tippy-toes!

1 Where does My Melody live?

a) Madagascar
b) Mari Land
c) Mexico

2 Who does this belong to?

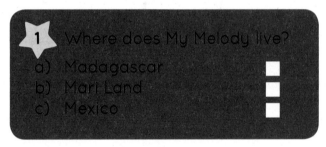

a) Charmmy Kitty
b) Hello Kitty
c) Chococat

3 Unjumble this anagram.

PROPIKE

a) Chococat
b) Keroppi
c) Keromi

4 Find the Sanrio character hiding inside the letterbox.

H	K	E	O	C	I
N	S	K	I	P	M
J	M	Z	L	T	O
D	R	Y	G	U	R
V	B	V	Q	A	U
K	X	F	M	J	K

5 What is my name?

a) Truck
b) Lorry
c) Karr

6 What sort of pet does Badtz-Maru have?

a) Pochi, a crocodile
b) Poochi, a puppy
c) Pandaba, a panda cub

7 What can Chococat do with his whiskers?

a) Play a tune
b) Pick up juicy bits of news
c) Tickle his friends

8 Which Sanrio character keeps a secret diary?

a) Kuromi
b) My Melody
c) Charmmy Kitty

9 Who is Flat's best friend?

a) Hello Kitty
b) Badtz-Maru
c) My Melody

10 Who is known worldwide for this adorable accessory?

a) Hello Kitty
b) Kuromi
c) My Melody

Don't forget to check your answers on page 93!

ANSWERS

PAGE 12–13
Nature Spotting

Hello Kitty has a lot of friends in the forest... like Joey the mouse and Lorry the squirrel!

PAGES 30
Tangled Lines

1. c.
2. d.
3. b.
4. a.

PAGE 31
Picture Perfect

Part 2 is covered.

PAGE 41
Trail of Hearts

PAGES 44–45
XO's Mind Muddlers

Puzzle 1:
1. Meet me at the skate park in one hour.
2. The answer to homework question number 2 is 100.
3. Let's buy Chococat a new collar for his birthday.
4. Last night I dreamt I was a cowboy.

Puzzle 2: 5 and 7 are the same.

Puzzle 3: 1. b., 2. c., 3. a., 4. d.

Puzzle 4: His fave food is Sushi

Puzzle 5: Panther, polar bear, prawn, parrot, pig, python, panda, pony, peacock, pelican, poodle etc

PAGE 49
Picture Perfect

1. Pandaba.
2. A cactus.
3. Hana-maru.
4. Bowling ball and skittles.
5. Pochi.

The jumbled up friend is Pandaba.

PAGE 54–55
Hippity Hoppity Puzzles

1. **Odd object out:**

   1.   2.   3.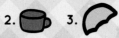

2. **Croaky counting:** 43 Keroppis.
3. **Letter jumble:** TERUTERU.
4. **Memories of Donut Pond**
   1. Red and white.
   2. Three.
   3. She is riding on a sledge.
   4. A snowman.
5. **Crazy for Keroppi:** There are lots of words that can be made, but here are a few to get you started... CROAK, PRIZE, ROOF, FORK, COOKERY.
6. **Gone fishin':**

PAGE 64
Terror Trail

Number of cobwebs: 15.
Number of spiders: 10.
Number of bats: 8.

PAGE 65

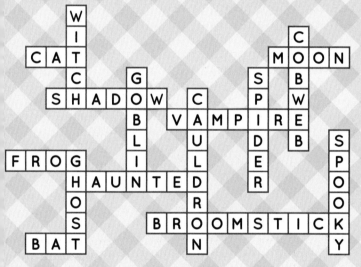

PAGE 70
Graffiti Spotting

PAGE 71
Picture Perfect

Shadow 2 is the same.

PAGE 79
Style Queen

True or False

1. True.
2. False.
3. Fale.
4. True.
5. False.
6. True.
7. True.

PAGES 86-87
Sanrio Box Bonanza

True or False

1. True.
2. True.
3. False.
4. True.
5. True.
6. True.
7. False.
8. False.
9. True.
10. False.
11. False.
12. True.

PAGES 88-89
Picked and Mixed!

PAGES 90-91
Quick 'n' Cute Quiz

1. b.
2. a.
3. b.
4. Kuromi.

H	K	E	O	C	I
N	S	K	I	P	M
J	M	Z	L	T	O
D	R	Y	G	U	R
V	B	V	Q	A	U
K	X	F	M	J	K

5. b.
6. a.
7. b.
8. a.
9. c.
10. c.
11. a.